Psychedelic Horror Press
Virginia, USA

www.psychedelichorrorpress.com
psychedelichorrorpress@gmail.com

Interior Design by Nicholaus Patnaude

Interior Illustrations by Thuy Vi Pham
www.2villustration.com

ISBN 978-0-578-19253-6

First Edition

PHP - 002

Bonespin Slipspace

by

Leo X. Robertson

Praise for
Bonespin Slipspace
by Leo X. Robertson

"I have never in my life been exposed to a more fascinatingly bizarre story—and I've been exposed to some pretty damn fascinating and bizarre stories in my day! Buy this damn book! Now!" – Michael Alig, star of *Glory Daze* and central subject of the film *Party Monster*

"Forget mind-bending ... this is a mind-twisting read, this is a mind-corkscrew, this is mind-macrame, unraveling and re-knotting with greater complexity at every turn of the page."
–Christine Morgan, The Horror Fiction Review

"Fun for the whole family, if you're the Manson Family" – Danger Slater, author of *Puppet Skin* and *I Will Rot Without You*

"An endearing thrill ride full of suspense and disgust and all the chaos conjured when oddity, horror and fantasy bump uglies while the rubbers hang out in the nightstand." – *Unnerving Magazine*

Blackburn

I'm nine and it's the third year in a row Dad's taken me to the Freak Show. Three times my jaw has fallen agape at its airbrushed demons, skulls with bat's wings, brick effect on painted metal and portraits of familiar monsters from films I'm way too young to have seen.

We've been patient, waited in the extra-long queue for seats right at the front—Dad insists on only the best experience.

Now it's our turn. A teenager ushers us into our seats.

'This time maybe you'll be brave enough to open your eyes, eh Kingsley Jr?' he says.

With one hand I grip his battered arm, fingers caressing his cuts. In my other hand I grip the sharpened Transformers pencils he won me at the raffle. The carriage twists up to the top floor: Day-Glo Bela Lugosi, snarling yellow fangs of a werewolf, pallid mask of a fictional serial killer. I look over the plastic balustrade and Styrofoam hawks to the kids below as they whisper to their parents who catch my eye: they wonder if the ride's appropriate for their own kids that dip in and out the line for tickets. In the background, a weight-balanced wheel of screaming seats spins loops of colour, tilting like a pendulum.

We push through spray-painted dungeon doors and I hear a pre-record-ed demon cackle as we slip through clear strip curtains to the darkness

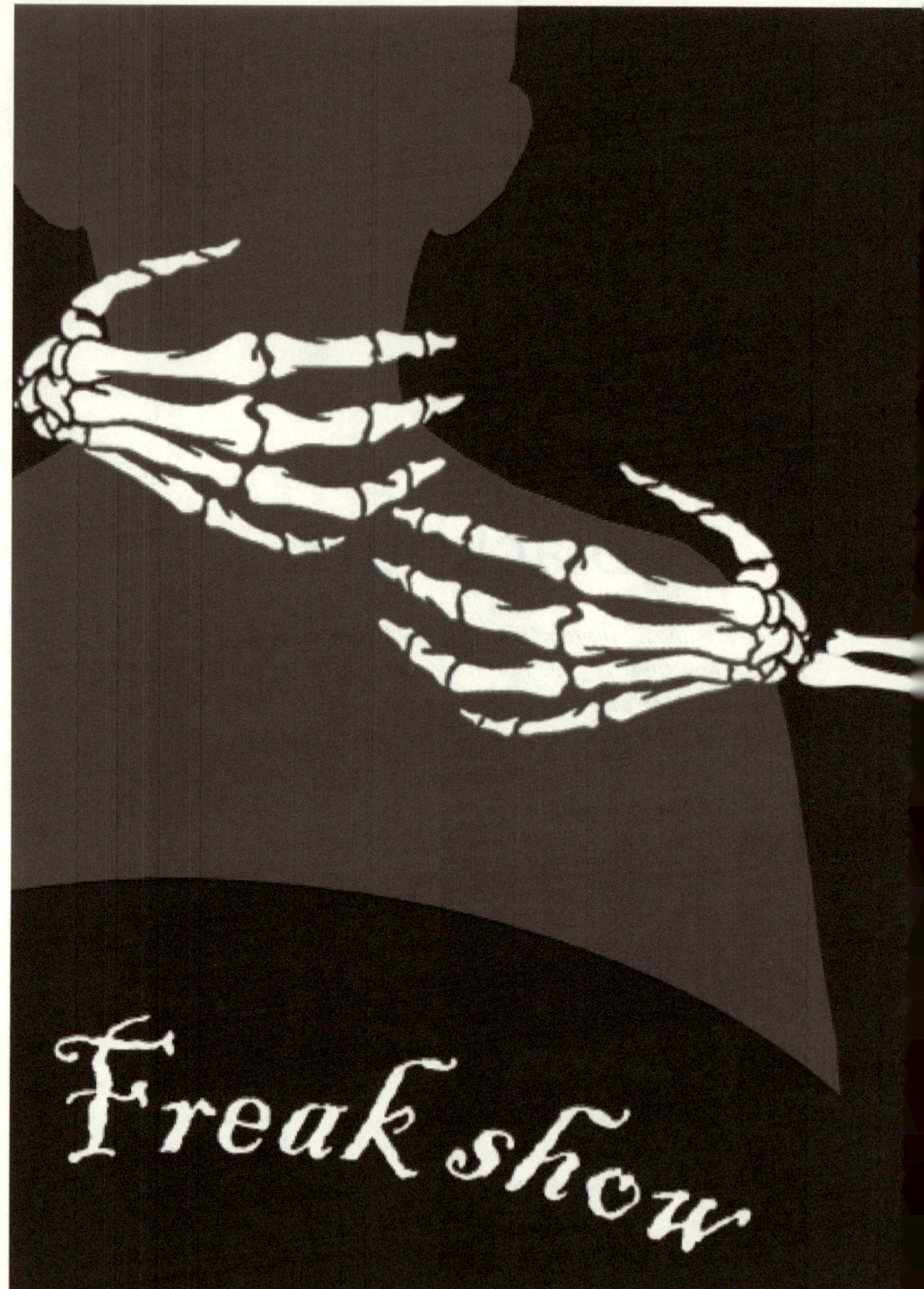

Freak show

beyond.

This year's the year I can do it.

I hear the ratchet crank of the carriage as we lock in place and tilt back, heading upwards, building momentum for the imminent fall through humid candyfloss air.

His hand's on my thigh now, creeping up.

Release.

We speed down the drop, careen to the right and a bat's head, the size of a car, slides in and out, beaming its glowing red eyes at us and just as we're about to slam into its face it rises up and puffs pneumatic hisses of compressed air on our necks from its coke can-sized nostrils.

I stay lucid for this, for the tableaux of a skeleton cook stirring his steaming bony broth, the man-sized mechanised rat howling from its synthetic gutter, the kids dressed in black body stockings with their glow-in-the-dark skeletons glued on the front caressing my neck with cold hands, Dad's jerky grip on my knee to see if he can jump a scare outta me, the automatic pistols ejaculating gouts of water from the mouths of mummy masks. I can always keep my eyes open for this. I want to.

Our carriage slows and we enter the stretch of track with its warped mirrors and the lights dim to reveal hologram ghouls behind the glass. The teenagers in their suits have gone and no hysterical laughter track accompanies Dad and me. For the next one hundred and one hippopotamuses, it's only our distorted reflections and us. Dad's hand starts wandering to its familiar places.

Every year before, I closed my eyes and left my body, left it behind for him.

He looks at me and licks his lips.

'You're scared, boy,' he says.

With a possessed hand I jab a pencil right into the fleshy muscle between his thumb and forefinger, and now I'm twisting it with the might of both my hands. One grips the shaft of the thing and the other is a fist kneading the tip into his tough flesh. As a reflex, his hand grips harder.

He screams a scream I hear echoing through my years, pre-recorded as it is into my psyche.

'Son's being brave now Dad,' I say, slamming a second pencil into his

7

windpipe, the wheeze of it as familiar as the background sucking of an
air conditioner.
    'You close your eyes. You dream.'

Rudy

Tammy fans the lime green tickets in front of her like a burlesque performer. They've got a cheap retro design: pixellated ghouls, a *Scream* mask, a black cat. Ollie's gotten hold of a dot matrix printer somehow.

She's already dressed and ready to go: red heels— eschewing our standard matching black Doc Martens— tartan skirt, black top, red hair and lips, and her pale brown coat made from real fox fur. Who knows how many weekdays she's already been wearing the same thing? Her weekends begin on Wednesdays. I wish she'd keep inviting me to all her events, even though we both know I'd decline every time.

'Suspicious that Ollie sent the tickets to you,' I say.

'We were friends too.' She heads upstairs and turns on her pre-game playlist, shouting down at me. 'We were the three Violent Femmes. The three... help me out here: all my favourite bands have more than three.'

'Violent Femmes is fine. Neither of us have spoken to Ollie in like three years.' I shuffle my bedding to the foot of the stairs so we can hear each other and I sit down on it. I reach across to my grandma's big overstretched handbag— which I

carry around with me like a bindle— and grab at my laptop, opening it up and bringing up my typical tabs: Brianna's fashion blog, Jorge's music review channel, *Vice*, and so on. I flick through each of them with glazed eyes, my friends competing for my attention.

'Are you sad he didn't send the tickets to you?' she says.

'Of course. I'd have torn them up and we wouldn't be having this discussion.'

Hey! Brianna's posted some scanned-in Polaroids from final year. Written on the bottom is *RUDY AND OLLIE, KINGS OF SLUT-FEST, 11/13*. I don't know what "Slut-fest" is. Looking down, I'm wearing the same torn black jeans and leather jacket with the shoulder spikes I put in myself for some fashion show or other before making off with the clothes afterwards. In the pictures, my blonde hair's tied back in a ponytail and I guess Alexandra or someone'd glued baby antlers to my forehead. That was me: Rudy the coke-nosed loser. Ollie's also out of it of course, big shark eyes behind his rimless professor glasses with the rounded lenses. He's wearing a stripy vest and chinos.

Manchester School of Art: the best memories aren't for us to remember.

'He's probably just chuffed to have a job, babes,' she says.

'Fine,' I say, 'so you think he's trying to prove something to us?'

Having curled her hair, Tammy comes back downstairs. 'Who cares? It's at Blackburn Manor, Rudy!'

'What?! I would never go there!'

'Oh, psssht.' She flicks a hand at me and looks at herself in a Barbie pocket mirror. 'Me and you don't even know where we're gonna be in half a year, let alone have the patience to wait that long to get into the Manor.'

'So say on the off chance I even did feel like seeing Ollie ever again, I'd have to do it while being waterboarded or fed dog food?'

11

'I mean…'

Tammy sits on the opposite side of the room from me, on a pillow with no cover that's beside the back door. It must be damp, and I have to watch her trail her mouse-bitten charger cable from the socket in the wall over what could be one of the floor's many oil stains or a puddle. Either way it's like watching a kid run up and down the train tracks while you scowl at an inattentive mother: nothing you can do but flinch and hate yourself for caring.

'The thing tonight's called "Bonespin",' she says. 'It's not like the Blackburn Manor Experience. It just takes place there. It could be pretty cool to check the place out and see if you'd go when it is the proper experience.'

She tosses this line off with the same tone she uses in all her blog posts, such as "Taking Pills I Find on the Floors of Canal Street Bars", "Getting Legally High in North Korea", "NSFL Pics of my BFFL's Body Mods."

'Are you telling me you had better plans tonight?' she continues. 'Out clubbing with your AA buddies?'

She scoffs and clicks at her laptop, not daring to look at me, gnawing at a finger to dull the cringe of her dig.

I guess I'm the idiot for deciding I don't wanna hear her say to strangers, 'That's the thing about Rudy: get him drunk and he'll pay for anything.' Doubly so for staying friends with her.

Her and Ollie were friends of mine from when I had such low self-esteem I didn't think I deserved better. I met Tammy on a dodgy bus after a club night out: she sat in the front window, talking to the driver, and I had to stop her from grabbing the wheel. But I thought she was outrageous fun. After that, she kinda adopted me and I became part of her circle.

It was fun back when we were in a student bar, sipping on snakebite and sitting in a group of ten, escalating each other's ironically snide comments, one after the other in a row.

'Rudy…' she says. 'I miss you. I miss this fun. I miss Ollie! When you guys broke up, we lost touch.'

I rub my eyes. 'Woe is us, then.'

She tilts her head and drops her jaw at my lameness.

'Okay! Fine! But I don't have to talk to him.'

'Yay!'

I don't mean I deserve better than Ollie: he was just great for the time.

I check his photography blog about once a week to see that indeed he's done nothing with it since 2011. One of the saddest things I learned from him is if you enjoy that person who's the life of the party, enjoy away, just don't go behind the curtain. Don't date him and coach him about his sexuality waverings or astounding laziness. And don't become his best friend and decide it would be fun to live with him in a dodgy area in an empty squat with oil spots on the bare concrete floor. With used futons with thin stained duvet covers to protect you from cold breezes through undetectable holes beneath the damp-peeled paint of skirting boards and window frames. With fingerprint- and genital-smudged smashed windows covered in duct-taped plastic bags, behind which is your back garden with rusty patio furniture overgrown with ivy and weeds where you and your friends smoke Camels, eat your one meal a day— either freezer-burnt or tastes of onion because of that one old wooden chopping board— while dreaming of hitchhiking to Paris.

Well, by all means do all of that. Learn the lessons yourself, gather enough semi-daring stories to wow your Tinder matches, escape.

Do escape though. Once, like me, your freelance web design affords you your own office space and sleeping bag, leave the squat and never return, or forever have your previous era friends dragging you to the same events, chipping away at your positive cash flow, keeping you where you are.

The walk to Blackburn Manor's some Wes Anderson shit: frosty winds crust week-old snow hard, mounds of it sparkling beneath the streetlights. Gingerbread-style houses up the rocky hills flicker orange lights in their windows: they seem hollow somehow, cardboard boxes beaming out the yellow glow of a single incandescent bulb. The firs are so perfectly flecked with white it's like they've been sprayed with some decorative chemical foam. On either side of us, beyond blandly painted picket fences are plastic-slatted houses in red, white and gold.

Soon we pass the houses and beside us is a crumbling wall with square stubs of rusted metal poking out. We step over it into the muddy grass beyond, into the graveyard.

In the distance are the white fountains of sparklers: they rush back and forth behind mausoleums, and the mausoleums have circular glowsticks slung over their spires and crosses. The graves we walk past are eroded mounds like tooth nubs. Peering into the mausoleums on either side of me, through their arched doorways, punks fuck girls up against the walls of caskets. I look straight ahead again.

We pass ornate sepulchres and discover a wet field bounded by four large floodlights with speakers at their sides. There's a DJ in the centre and a loose donut of revellers around him, dressed either Rocky Horror-style or H&M punk rocker.

And there's the manor, complete with crenellated battlements, fading gargoyles, parapets branching into more parapets, all in sooted limestone. Some old rich guy's castle it used to be. God knows who this Blackburn chappy is— no secret how he could afford it though, what with the success of the Manor Experience.

'I'm gonna cut you, fucker!'

A hand clamps over my eyes and I feel a penknife press against my throat. I gulp and my Adam's apple scrapes against the blade.

Tammy laughs. The hand releases from my eyes but slides around my neck as a grinning face comes from behind me.

'Some people shake hands, Ollie,' I say.

'Come on, Rudy,' Tammy says. 'It's just Ollie! He wasn't gonna hurt you.'

'I didn't know it was him.'

Ollie's face falls and he rubs his bobbly black stubble. 'I'm so sorry, Rudy. I was just joking around.'

Tammy places a hand on Ollie's shoulder and eyes me up. 'Don't be sorry just because this one can't take a joke.'

Ollie smiles faintly. 'Good to see you both anyways. Here, Tammy.' He takes some little yellow papers from the front pocket of his leather jacket. 'Here's your drink tickets. Bar's over there. Go nuts!'

'Cheers Ollie! I'll be back with your Jack and Coke. And Rudy's lemonade.'

'Looking for some pills tonight?' Ollie says.

'I'm sober: no drinking, smoking, drugging— none of it.'

'When?'

'Like a few months after we split.'

'Oh. Wise choice my man. If you had a time like mine those first few months after... I was a total write-off.'

I smile. 'Exactly. I used up my life's substance quota quick smart.'

'Substance quota! How'd you come up with this shit? Still... thanks for coming.'

'Congrats on the job.'

Ollie takes a cigarette from behind his ear and lights it. 'Was my bro that hooked me up with it.'

I look around. 'Alex isn't here tonight, though?'

'He's back in jail already.'

'Already?'

'Yeah, man. For good this time, they think.'

'Sorry to hear that.'

'Shouldn't be, mate. It's all good.'

'But he was working at Blackburn Manor? That should've tipped the police off as it is!' I try to laugh. 'Oh shit: you work

15

here, don't you? I-I just figured you were working in events in general or something. I couldn't see you… here. How is it?'

He slaps his hands onto the spikes in my shoulders, leaving them there. 'I've found my thing, Rudy. You always nagged me about that, and now that I've found it, I know exactly what you were saying, about earning your own keep, being stable and that.' His hands drop to his sides.

I rub the back of my neck. 'Hey, if it works for you, I guess…'

'Because Alex worked here, I got to skip the waiting time. I just told him a week I was free: that's all I had to do.'

'What do they do?'

Ollie ushers me away from the field, up against the manor's wall. 'I'm not really allowed to talk about it. But you're not gonna tell anyone else, are you? Well, I was staying in that flat— our flat by the campus? I signed this contract and had to give them a house key. One night I can't sleep. I'm convinced there's an intruder in the flat. Like, I've been hearing noises, someone creeping about in the attic, for hours. But I'm watching TV, by myself, and I'm too afraid to check. Now, they don't tell you any of this when you sign or it wouldn't be a surprise. Finally, I've the nerve to get up from the living room, bolt across the corridor in the dark and fall into bed, wrapping myself up with the sheets. I hear something groaning my name— "Olliiieeee…"—again and again. Not loud enough for me to be sure I'm really hearing anything. I see this mask, this big rubber clown mask with glow-in-the-dark makeup around the eyes and mouth. This is the week I agreed upon with the Manor. You would think that the experience you pay for is for actors to act out your darkest fantasies, but these guys are legit: there's no character to break'

Ollie's telling me this story, smoking his cigarette, and I picture him in bed, in our bed near the campus. In my mind I'm the clown, towering over his naked, sweaty body, and I feel myself getting an erection.

'So I'm frozen in bed and I feel this hand creeping up my

16

leg.' Two fingers walk an itsy bitsy spider up my thigh, across the bare patches in my jeans and across my flesh. 'I hear laughter. The clown jumps.'

A hand pounces on my chest and I laugh.

'He jumps on me. He presses a hand on my mouth.'

Ollie clamps his hand over my mouth.

'He shoves a bag over my head.'

His hand comes behind my head and he strokes my hair, getting closer.

'He ties me up.'

His hand lowers itself into the small of my back as he presses our hips together.

'I feel more guys grabbing onto me.'

He grabs my arse.

'They cart me out the flat.'

The cigarette drops from his lips into the grass and we kiss. I taste the ash in his mouth, but I don't care. I grip him back.

'I missed you, man,' he says.

Fuck.

We kiss longer, harder. Kids dressed as ghouls cheer as they pass us. Soon we let go of each other, press our heads against the wall and look into each other's eyes.

Ollie presses fingertips to his temple and lets his hand float away from his head. 'Honestly, it was such a mind-fuck that it wasn't until they got me out the van and tied me to a chair and I heard a guy shout "Welcome to Blackburn Manor, maggot!" that I really believed it was them. And I still don't know how long they were in the flat or how long I was maybe imagining them creeping about.'

'Holy fuck, Ollie,' I say. My heart swells with lust. '... Then what did they make you do?'

'For sure I can't tell you what goes on in the Manor. But I can tell you this.' He presses his hand to my chest and my breathing deepens. 'It changed me. It's not something I would wish on you or Tammy or anyone. But I needed it. I must have known I needed it or I wouldn't have signed up. Alex must have known I needed it. And now I get to do what they did to me, to other people.'

I think hard about asking for a demo, but I keep quiet.

'You lose your mind in the Manor, Rudy. You lose your ego. Like acid, but... it's real. You know it's real the whole time. That you've really left yourself.'

I fold my arms. 'Yes, well that sounds suitably fucking terrifying and I'm glad to continue never having done that. And I won't ever understand those who do.' On that point I'm wavering. I look over Ollie's head. 'Where did Tammy head off to?' I'm shouting now: the DJ's playing some splintered unnameable genre of blippy stuff.

'I can barely hear you over the new wave tech-step,' he says. 'Tammy? She's probably off into the mausoleum with some dealer by now, no? Come inside with me. That's the bit these plebs can't see.' He winks and links his arm in mine.

If the rumours are to be believed, Blackburn Manor belonged to some local gangster in the early twentieth century. While fuelled by some brutal early version of cough syrup akin to today's bath salts, he blasted the head off anything in the manor that had a head, including himself. And more recently, before Kingsley Blackburn got a hold of it, one of those punk bands, lauded more for their public disruption than their shitty two-minute-max tunes, squatted in it. The lead singer kidnapped triplets, girls, and the burned corpses of two of them were found in the basement. That bit was true, and while passing a tray of coke around our squat, we once pretended to be the grown-up third triplet.

I give my ticket to the attendant in the foyer. She wears a leather corset, her pierced breasts on display, each containing a horizontal and vertical sliver of metal like a toothpick. She's only lit with black-light and I can't tell if it's just a shadow or blood dripping from her nipples.

19

I hear moaning beneath me and look down to see that I'm standing on an identically pierced breast that rises up out of a hole in the floor. I grip onto Ollie and look around. The foyer's floor's covered in holes in the black plywood. The holes are lined with green, pink, yellow or blue glow-in-the-dark paint, and some of the flesh itself is also painted: hands, vaginas, erect penises, non-gender-specific buttocks.

I step off the breast and try to imagine how all these people are configured beneath the floor: the density of human components looks too high to be possible let alone comfy.

We walk through and to the hall. Ollie bends down as if to grab one of the penises, but he turns to me and grins and sees my face and his hand jerks away before he touches it.

In the hall's a maze of more black plywood that takes up the full floor. Now I'm getting the full plasticky body paint and popper smell in the muggy air. A narrow path left and right leads to the black velvet-lined stairs to the upper floor. Large white candles are glued with their own wax to the marble bannisters. Three wooden platforms jut out over the rim of the upper floor: they're circular, and on the bottom of them are painted psychedelic eyes. Each platform has its own pole and dancer. As I follow my line of sight up the pole, I see naked men strapped by the feet to the ceiling, rusty cages chained over their heads, flailing to the beat of major key techno.

I reach out and grip Ollie's hand.

'Dude, if this is freaking you out, you can just go. Seriously. But… I wish you wouldn't.'

'It's cool,' I say. 'We've seen worse, right?' No way. 'I've just never been to an event like this sober.'

'I'll lead the way, then,' he says, heading straight for the maze's entrance.

'Whoa whoa,' I say. 'Shouldn't we go upstairs?'

'Maybe later,' he shouts. 'I don't think you can handle what's up there yet. Let me show you what's after this maze.'

'You know the way through, right?'

'Just don't let go of me!'

There are more holes cut out of the walls, between TVs with big close-up videos of twitching eyeballs. Through the empty holes I can see that behind the walls are gaps just big enough for a very thin person. The width of the gaps must vary: surely the empty holes are just there to mess with your perception as much as the ones with the arms coming out of them at full stretch to grab at your neck, or the more erect penises bobbing about whack-a-mole style, or the glory holes in which eyeballs twitch, or the feet and knees, or the breasts flopping out and brushing our cheeks. Some are live and warm, others are cadaver blue and icy cold. Two girls with multi-coloured dreadlocks, which look like they're made out of fabric, have pulled up their gas masks and they're making out while arms emerge from the walls and caress them. Their tutus brush me as Ollie leads the way.

'It's calmer in the rooms beyond here— I promise!'

'We'll surely have earned it by then.'

We twist past bleeding appendages and TVs playing shock videos of self-performed gender reassignment surgery, faecophiliac porn, autoerotic needle play. I'm so disoriented that by the time we get out the maze and stumble through its narrowing exit with lubricated walls, brushing past more body parts of more disturbed individuals, I realise there's no way for me to get out the manor without Ollie's help.

Calming music infuses the red room beyond the maze. Waiters and waitresses wear red silk kimonos and hold trays of white powder. Lady guests wear cocktail dresses and men wear suits, and from their collars and sleeves I can see worn black tattoos. The place has a green room vibe where the manor's twenty or so members of the glitterati can chat at a low volume and look mildly fed up. One gentleman looks particularly "raj": he's staring at me. He stands up from the red leather bench lining the wall and approaches us, my eyes locking onto his.

'Mr Blackburn!' Ollie says. 'I... didn't think you'd be here.'

Blackburn's an enormously muscly man. As he gets closer, I see he has that steroid-induced bad skin, the kind that looks like you could just wipe it right off someone's face. But it's a privilege to see him: there are no publicly available images of him.

Ollie holds his hand out but Blackburn continues to stare at me.

'Didn't think I'd attend my own party?' he says. 'Who's this?' He speaks with a Scottish accent: from Ayr, I think.

'This is my mate Rudy,' Ollie says. 'He's one of my guests this evening.'

'Has he signed the non-disclosure?'

Ollie stays silent.

'I'll take him to do it now,' Blackburn says, forcefully shoving away two opulent ladies in matching ballroom gowns on either side of him, whose expressions remain the same, while their speaking volumes increase a little as the shove forces the air out them.

'Is that really necessary?' Ollie says, his hand still clinging to mine. I squeeze his harder. 'I can vouch for him. Please, just consider any fault of his a fault of mine and you can punish me instead if you need to...' His voice fades below the noise of the music.

'Oliver: you of anyone know the importance of keeping what goes on in here a secret.'

'It's my top priority.'

'Good. It's not necessary for you to come with us.'

'I'd be more comfy if—'

'It's two seconds. A bit of paper. Come with me,' Blackburn says to me.

'I don't want to cause any fuss,' I say.

'No fuss. Over in a minute. Just come with me.'

'We're gonna go,' Ollie says to me.

I frown and look to him.

'I don't care if you stay or go, but you're not doing anything else until he comes with me and signs a non-disclosure.' He shoots Ollie the unmistakable look of a pugnacious alpha gorilla demanding a subordinate volunteer its meat.

He tugs mine and Ollie's hands apart and grips me too firmly by the shoulder, ushering me towards a red leather-padded door in the wall. He reaches up and pushes upon one of the buttons in the leather: it clicks and swings backwards, revealing a barely lit staircase with a steel door beneath fluorescent light at the top. He pushes a hand into my back while the other grips my shoulder as he leads me up the stairs. He types a code into a pad by the door so it opens.

Inside's what he referred to as his office, but it's more like a hotel room. There's a desk— a sheet of steel jutting out the wall so thin it looks like you can cut yourself on it— with metal stools in front of it, and beside are steel filing cabinets. But there's also a big double bed with black sheets askew, an opaque shower curtain cordoning off a large tiled corner of the room with a drain in the centre, and an Edwardian bureau— looks to be mahogany and has a gold-tasselled key hanging out of it. Across the walls are clusters of oil portrait paintings that overlap each other and dangle precariously from drooping nails. They're from every era: from the old and decaying and cracked-like wood, to the cartoon-like, to the lumpy-textured abstract, always in muddy colours, always stoic and resolute faces, on a background of pure black.

He goes to the bureau and unlocks it, removing a folder. He gestures for me to sit on a black velvet couch in the dark space opposite the bed.

'Drink?' he says.

'Water?'

He laughs.

The single bedside table is a safe. He turns the knob on the front and it opens up. It's a fridge of sorts with little mini-bar-style bottles inside, and on one side are neatly lined up plastic bags with powders and pills inside. With one hand, he elegantly grabs two Famous Grouses and a bag of powder. He throws one of the bottles my way and walks to the desk, tipping the powder on it and removing a safety razor from the bag, cutting the powder into lines.

'If you could just give me the form to sign…' I say.

He looks insulted, dehydrated furrows cutting into his fore-head and from down either side of his nose. His skin has the uniform tan and colour achieved by sunbeds in winter. He pulls down a flap from the metal wall above the desk to reveal a mir-ror and he checks that his gelled black hair's all in place. While still looking in the mirror, he kicks one of the stools towards me. I flinch at the hammer-like slamming sound it makes, clat-tering across the floor, arriving in front of me.

'I have the form here,' he says, tapping the desk before nearly bashing his nose on it as his head skids across a line of powder, snorting it up.

He sits on the stool and his legs trap me against the couch on either side. He holds out the powder on his finger for me, and when I stay still, he pushes it into my mouth and rubs it against my gums, massaging them. Amongst other things, his finger tastes salty.

'There you go,' he says. 'What was your name again?'

'Rudy,' I say. His finger's still in my mouth.

'Rudy.' He takes the finger out and sucks it. 'To be here tonight, ordinarily you have to sign up for the six-hour experience, wait six months, and complete the experience. Less than one percent of entrants make it. You can only imagine, then, what things you may be privy to within these walls tonight. Tell me, Rudy: are you interested in what we're offering?'

Blackburn looks like he can and will knock me out with one punch and use my body every which way. I smirk like I might let him.

'What'll happen if I don't sign?'

He shrugs. 'I can't let you roam around free, I'll say that much.'

"What do you mean by "what this place offers?"'

'I'll show you. Anyway, this is all formality. Let's get better acquainted. How do you know Ollie?'

'He's my boyfriend.'

'No he isn't.'

'Close friend.'

'No.'

'We went out, three years ago.'

He stares at me intensely in response.

'We had a great time, though.'

'What else.'

I drink the rest of the bottle. 'Nothing else. Great time, separate ways.'

'No no no… you have to give me something.' He presses a hand to the side of his face, leaning the elbow on one thigh. He's got dead shark eyes, just like Ollie on pills.

'I thought we had a great time. But Ollie's a blank slate. He has nothing. He charms his way into other people's lives and forces them to rely on him emotionally, financially—'

'Sexually?'

'Some of his exes, surely. We have a club.'

Blackburn grins and a gravelly laugh spills out of him. I feel guilty for kissing Ollie again and then for gossiping about him.

'Sounds like you're ready for a real man, then,' Blackburn says. 'Sign and we'll find you one.'

He hands me a pen and the agreement. He turns around so I can use his back to sign. Beneath his shirt I can feel crater-like scars, cuts, fresh burns, lumpy and crusted. I sign quickly and drop the form to the floor. He spins around on the stool and grabs my hair, tugging my head back.

'Good,' he says.

His tongue comes out and pushes at my lips. He holds my jaw open and licks the inside of my mouth. I don't feel he wants me to engage in the kiss with him. I'm kissed upon. I reach out my arms and stroke his sides.

'Rudolph the red-arsed stranger.' Eugh. 'Wait here.'

From the safe, he takes out an iPad and returns to the stool. The room seems to get colder.

'You've earned my trust, Rudy. Now I can show you this.'

He shows me a photo on the screen. A man lies flat on an autopsy table and a woman on top's inserting his dick inside her. She has fresh piercings made with more of those metal slivers marking her chest, breast and arms, blood streaming down all over her. She wears heavy makeup and she's grinning. He has gashes cut out of his stomach from which bulbs of intestines bulge His eyes are closed either in ecstasy or death. Another naked man lies flat over the stomach of the guy on the autopsy table, and a third naked man holds his dick and it becomes clear he's about to climb onto the table and fuck one of the stomach gashes, as the man lying flat is likely already doing.

'This was Monday,' Blackburn says. 'Are you interested in this?'

A voice comes from deep within me that doesn't sound like mine anymore. It's a mirror of Blackburn's voice, extracted from me: 'Yes,' the voice hisses. But I agree.

The next photo's in a similarly dank dungeon-like place with crumbling brick walls. The photo's dense with naked flesh, a seraglio of fuckery. First my eyes focus on a naked man pressed up against the wall, his wrists bound to rusted metal rings embedded in the mortar. An Asian lady, again with heavy make-

28

up, is pulling out his bottom lip and draws a scalpel across it: she's halfway through cutting the lip off. The man's face is dead but his erection's at full mast. Behind the woman is Blackburn, fucking her, his face turned as if talking to someone behind the camera.

'Ollie took this one,' he says. 'And I took this next one of Ollie.'

Ollie kneels on a black floor, wearing just his trademark leather cap and glasses. A black dick's deep in his mouth. His hands are bound with rope in front of him, eyes behind the glasses looking in completely different directions. Across his dark skin are big wedge-shaped scars that shine against the camera's flash.

'His brother,' Blackburn says, laughing his gravelly laugh again.

Now I had an erection too. 'That's Alex's dick he's sucking?'

'It sure is.'

'How did that ever happen?'

'Alex has been doing this to Ollie since forever. Eventually Ollie cut ties. But that was only last year, so he was probably up to this the whole time you and him were together.'

'Why didn't he tell me?' I say. 'I would have joined.'

Blackburn bites his lip. 'Ollie was desperate for a job and Alex wanted him back. Alex is one of my confidants, so I got Ollie a job here. This photo was taken some time during hour six of Ollie's initiation. It's doubtful that he's forming memories by this point, what with all the sensory deprivation, blood loss and humiliation he's already been through.'

'Does he know this happened?'

'Sure, but it happened like a dream. A dream he was thankful for, clearly. And so are the countless other people Ollie has helped to indulge in their fetishes of choice. It's the therapy they've always been looking for.'

'Ollie told me Alex is in prison, now.'

'I got him sprung. You'd be surprised how many Manorites

29

you pass in the street every day.' He begins to take off his shirt and across his tight muscles I see the pock marks of cigarette burns, oozing self-sutured wounds, a wrap of bloody bandages across his abdomen. 'Alex is very important to me. I hope he soon becomes important to you, latest recruit.'

'What are you going to do to me?' I say as he slips his hands beneath my jacket and begins to remove it.

'What you've always dreamed of.'

Tammy

'You're Ollie's brother!'

'Sure am.'

'I always wanted to have a threesome with Ollie and Rudy when they were going out.'

'Me too.'

'Hah. You're fucking sick.'

I'd spotted Alex at the rave outside, not only because he stood still, staring at me, but he looked like an older version of Ollie. I can't tell who modelled their appearance after whom: the round glasses, leather cap and jacket, the red skinny jeans… Whatever: Alex is an Ollie I can fuck. Perfect.

He holds my hand and takes me round the back of the manor where he's got his own tent. I hike up my tartan skirt a little while pretending to check if I got my fur coat muddy. Behind the manor, the grass around the unmarked graves is littered with identical pop-up tents, glowing green, yellow and pale pink, like fireflies.

We reach the entrance of his tent. It's lined with pillows. From behind, he grabs one of my shoulders and pushes me so I trip forwards, and he catches me with one hand on my belly,

31

shoving me in. I giggle and turn around to see that taped to the ceiling are black strings with bones tied to them.

'You're a fuckin' freak, Alex!'

'Oh yeah? Check this out.'

He lies on top of me and pushes my hands back, the pillows parting so they're pressed against the tent's floor's thin membrane that's cold and feels as wet as the grass beneath. My hands begin to warm and feel like they're superglued to the ground.

'What's this?' I say.

He doesn't reply. Instead, he's chanting something at a volume too low for me to hear. Doesn't sound like any language I've heard. Above me, the bones— a scapula, shinbone, breastbone, collarbone, the little hazelnut-sized ones in the hand, the broken ball joints from the leg and humerus— they begin to spin, gently at first like a mobile, but soon at a speed that the gentle wind outside can't be creating, knocking against each other with the hollow sound of dry wood. They are surely human and real, all of them.

I'm in a trance. As the bones move, I see their spinning path extrude into solid objects. Alex appears in front of me only in a series of images. He brings his face before me and it morphs into the faces of other people. Some of them I recognise: Ollie, an ex, my dad. Two balls pulse in and out of his temples, like bad knocks to the head at first, but soon they grow into pulsing horns, horns like bones covered in flesh.

I still can't move my hands. The music from outside grows, no longer indietronica but some kinda old heavy metal band I haven't heard of.

'I really love women's... sides,' Alex says.

'Uh... huh...' I say with the same slur of a drunk without any of the party in my head.

Alex pounces on top of me and sniffs up my sides, from my hip up to my armpit, and the motion of his nose pushes my top up so he can see my bra. He flicks off his cap and glasses and brings his face to my chest. I can smell the thick oil in his face and a spicy cologne. I feel the warm wet touch of his tongue in my cleavage, roaming around.

I scream. Deep sharp stabs cut my flesh in spirals as he nuzzles harder into me. Feels like knuckles hard on my scalp the way his chin digs into my ribs while he cuts me, a big, extended paper cut of a slice.

He gets up so I can see his face, but he isn't looking at me any longer. He's no longer here. He speaks louder, in tongues, in a voice that doesn't sound like his, and blood flows in a steady waterfall from his mouth down his chin and chest and spills over me, a warm red shower of it, an impossible flow of blood, spilling down onto my own blood. I'm still screaming.

His head shakes back and forth and blood flicks out in gobs all over my face, his tongue lolling out his mouth, split in two horizontal flaps by a blade in its centre that he must be using to cut me.

I wrestle my legs free from his and knee him in the balls. He jerks forwards and the blade in his tongue slips out and falls into my mouth. I turn to the side, choking as it slices my inner cheek. I grip it with my teeth, turning back to Alex— he's back in the tent with me: I can see it in his eyes— and with this blade, a little arrow tip-style thing, I make as if to head-butt him and sink the blade into his neck. He screams in that other voice and falls to his side, seizing. My hands are free. The bones stop spinning.

I get up and out of the tent and run through the network of other tents. I can see silhouettes of couples pulsing, of strings of bones and big candles. The music's a dull throb now. The tents, like birth canals, spill out strange creatures in black fluid: naked women screaming like crows with deep cuts all over their bodies, still fresh and red; men with goat's legs who run to stamp on a screaming woman's face, sticking out from the grass; a gimp wearing a bloody pig's head wrapped in barbed wire. Between the tents are naked crones with strings of grey

33

hair on their bald heads: they point towards me and laugh.

They spill out at me, running after me and grabbing at me, laughing. The ground splits and bulges of maggots in a honey-like fluid cover the grass. The sky turns a deep black as thousands of bat's wings all flutter as collectively loud as a tidal wave. In another pulse of the tents' light, all the demons become Alex, and the Alexes grow to the manor's height and disappear and reappear at their original size as witches and warlocks again, and the light becomes more intense and the tents grow to tipis with all kinds of creatures etched in black shadows engaged in weird, evil copulation.

I make it out of the manor's grounds and back to the streets that only an hour or so ago I'd walked with Rudy.

Where's Rudy?

Still my vision flashes between overlapping images: at first I can see those white, red, brown and grey houses with their picket fences; another flash and they're stripped of their walls, burnt-out hollows with rooms in states of decay, or simply square gardens of dirt, and out come dirty skeletons from the frozen earth, and I'm still running as zombies burst out of graves and the cars on the street melt and crumple and turn to rusty skeletons.

All returns to normal. Everything is silent. I slow my pace and keep walking, and a barrier of men in ragged clothing appear, blocking the street completely.

'What are we all doing here?' says the one in the middle. He's holding a long, broken piece of wood.

'You're trying to get me,' I say.

'Why?' he says.

'You want me to die.'

'Not yet.'

In a flash they're gone but all the houses have decayed again and on the burnt out floors of all the suburban houses are naked witches with grey skin getting buggered on scorched bed frames, warlocks getting blown while they laugh and play fiddles with buzzing hands.

I run.

Beyond these houses, fairground lights glow, the curve of a big wheel shining in the pre-dawn sky of orange and purple. Soon, the fairground is in full view, the houses parting to reveal it, empty but lit up, guarded by a moat.

I turn around and see an army of weird spirits lurching behind me, eyes glowing vomit yellow, giving chase. I run towards the bridge across the moat but there's a pile of burnt-out cars stacked up in front of it.

'God!'

They laugh their weird and twisted laughs as I kick off my heels and jump onto the first car, the coarse sand of the rust scraping my hands and knees. I scramble to my feet and climb onto the second, then the third car in the burnt pyramid: the weird monument to the Manor.

Claws sink into my ankle. I scream and grab at the empty window frame of a car door above me and it swings open, sending me back towards the horde, and further claws dig into me and drag me down. Still I cling to the empty window frame and the car slides out of the pyramid towards us.

'Fuck!'

Once I'm in the fairground, I'm safe. That's what the moat's for. The cars are stacked high from the border of one house to the other across the street, but I can see now that there's nothing beyond the water.

I kick and some of the claws release, taking chunks of my flesh with them. The car's about to fall, so I scramble my way inside and brace myself against its roof and floor. I tumble out and fall, crushing the demons beneath me.

The car's upside down and the creatures are scrabbling in. I get out the other side and try my ascent a second time, running fluidly up from car to car until I'm at the tower's top and the cars beneath are crawling with demons. Since they can build no obstruction beyond the bridge, the cars are lined up flat with

36

each other on the other side, which I can see looking down. I have to climb down the wall of cars.

I use the spaces between cars to gain footing and climb down using door handles, the nubs where wing mirrors used to be and empty window frames that cut into the bare soles of my feet. Above me, the demons can only watch, not daring to cross the water's threshold.

They screech. Some reveal their wings. Some blow fire. Together they begin to push the cars down on me.

A rusted shell of a car falls beside me with an empty howl, splashing into the water. I'm halfway down. To my right, another comes and bashes my hand out of place. I let go and fall the height of a four-car stack, landing on the stony bridge. The wall of cars above is curling towards me in a rusty wave. I crawl over the bridge, towards the open gates of the fairground. I turn on my back and look up, still shuffling backwards, and I'm beyond the water but not yet with the strength to stand up, and cars fall in a rain of metal. Exhausted, I lie down and hold an arm over my eyes.

The cars, crossing the water, dissolve like a magic trick.

I grab onto the turnstile and raise myself up to look at the demons that grow like hair from the car pyramid.

I give them the finger.

'Hah! You stupid cunts!' I turn and raise my skirt up. 'You'll never get a piece of this now!'

You're not safe yet, says a voice in my head. It sounds like Alex.

The demons jeer and scream and cackle, but I turn my attention to the fairground before me, eager to carry on my night's journey home, but first I fall to my knees and stop to scream. I beat my head against the tarmac and tug at my hair. From a pocket in my skirt, I remove a baggie of coke and spill the contents on the floor with a shaking hand, snorting up as much of the dust that doesn't clump and melt.

The smell of cold vomit, of old soft drink stains, carrying through the chill evening air… It's not a fair I see. It's the composite of so many fairs from my memory. The big wheel's the size it looked to me as a kid, the hall of mirrors not a cheap chamber of bashed plastic but a fearful infinite space. The many stands with their rhubarb and custard-coloured awnings, their coconuts, their milk bottles and hoops, their water pistols and monkey targets, their dartboards and their raffles, they all glow with the neon colours of my youth against a wavering, shivering oppressing night. The pink teddies and the red Coca Cola footballs and etch-a-sketch keyrings: here they all are in this black wasteland, all these parts of a fair assembled in one place, discrete objects from times that no longer exist. Not a memory but a broken lens from an imagined time.

The tarmac beneath my feet is soaked with damp. It's nice and cool against the cuts on my feet. I wipe the blood from my chest. I can feel two spiral cuts like opposing goat's horns cut into my flesh.

It's cold. I left my coat in the tent. Behind me, the demons and their rusted cars dissolve into darkness.

My path is chosen for me. While it looks like I'm free to roam wherever, I can do nothing but enter the hall of mirrors. An invisible force gives the illusion of freedom, like the hall itself. It draws my path towards the hall.

The booth at the front is empty. I wince at the big yellowy bulbs that shine with an eerie strength you sometimes see in lights just before lightning's about to strike. I follow the painted signs to enter the hall.

I walk slowly through each prism. I lick my palm and clear the blood I see across my chest in the reflection and through the infinite space ahead of me, his image appears: a two-dimensional Alex, naked and stroking his dick aggressively, leering at me and grinning. I scream and bash my head against the wrong path, staggering forwards on bare feet. The floor feels like a wet tongue and I don't dare look down. Instead, I close my eyes and hold my hands out, feeling the walls to guide me beyond the mirrors. The walls melt into Alex's hard, fleshy stomach. My hands recoil at their touch. How is he here, beyond the water, in my memory's neon village?

My breathing's shallow and I feel pins and needles as oxygen leaves my extremities. I keep going. The walls become cold plastic again and I open my eyes. I'm trapped in a central hexagon and feel all around: a mirror on every surface, my bloodied self reflected a thousand-fold in harsh light.

'Noooo!' I spin around, screaming, tugging again at my hair, beating at the walls. 'I was free, Alex! I left you behind, you bastard!'

I slump to the floor, my tights torn in big holes. I stare at my cherry toenails poking through the material and beyond to my reflections. I turn around and around, and in one of the faces, I see behind myself, like I'm looking at myself in a new chamber. I wave my foot in front of me and the clone of me in the chamber in front does the same, so I kick at the wall, breaking the plastic. I shove my force against it and the plastic turns white with the stress. Leaning against the wall behind me, I kick with both feet and the plastic shatters.

Beyond is nothing, just darkness.

Pulling at the opening I've kicked in the wall, I make a hole big enough to climb through, and through I go, but the new dark chamber has no floor, and I fall and tumble.

I can't quite describe how I land. There's no thud, but the wind rushes past me and disappears, and I'm at the foot of The King's Circus, a "funhouse" I was too afraid to go all the way through when I was little. There was a rumour that a woman died on a conveyor belt that jerked back and forth: her hair got caught and a little summer student at the helm of the controls scalped her.

All Alex can do here is scare me. But I can do this. I walk past the booth: this time there's a headless female mannequin inside. I pay it no mind and push the turnstile, walking across the bridge in the black-lit chamber with glow-in-the-dark walls that spin around. Through the doorway at its end I see a witch's shadow as she walks past the wall of white stars at the end, dragging a girl's— my body by the hair. I look away, ashamed and scared, before I regain my grip on the handrails and carry on.

The next room's completely black again. I can feel the grid pattern of a metal floor beneath me. I feel for the walls. The floor collapses and I slide down, banging my head on the way, landing in a foam-padded basement. There it is: the floating mannequin head lit up in a box of mirrors behind a ladder I have to climb up to get out. My dad had said 'Just close your eyes, Tammy,' and he'd taken me under one arm and carted me up so I didn't have to see it. It's just a plaster cast of a face, continuously dripping white fluid coloured in different lights by the box. I grip the sides of the ladder and venture forwards with a foot on the bottom rung. I climb up and when my face is level with the head in the box, the mouth opens and it laughs 'Ahahaha!' and I scream again and a river of blood spews from its laughing mouth and fills the box, and as I run up the ladder, the struts begin to melt and sag beneath my feet until the strut at the very top splits in two completely. I use all the force in my arms to hoist myself through the hole in the floor above.

The arms of a King Kong statue move up and down to usher me towards a spiral slide of orange plastic. There used to be a teenager who would stand there and say 'If you're too scared to go on, just take this slide down and you can leave right now.' I can feel hot breath on my neck and the intuitive sensation of a hand in my personal space reaching towards me, so I run and sling myself into the slide and laughter echoes down the slide's tube behind me. I shiver and burst into tears when I land on the mat at the bottom. But I have to keep moving.

Now in front of me is a merry-go-round, a big ostentatious thing with painted horses, golden spiral poles and yellow and orange bulbs all over it, grinding some automatic organ music. It spins and beckons me gently, and I'm guided by the same force towards it. In the dark of night, it's a cylinder of white light.

41

I climb up the metal steps and hoist myself onto one of the horses and the organ music coming from the speakers above gets louder and speeds up, just like the horses themselves that course round faster and faster as I grip onto the spiral pole in front of me, and as the cheery music plays, so does Alex appear again, naked on the horse in front of me, then standing on the steps and glaring at me, and soon there are witches on every pole, tilting their heads back in ecstasy and moaning, and as we spin, just like a long exposure photograph, the lights all around form circles of red, yellow and white light, and the night spins around and around and I grip harder as the horse threatens to thrust me off, and we cycle through the night's hours together in a swirling, time-lapse circle, and soon the orange morning light spins around me and the paint of the merry-go-round rises into the air and flakes off, leaving hollow metal horse casts behind, the pole getting colder, the lights shattering and smashed glass flying out in all directions, and it's morning, and the fairground is gone, and the horses have lost their tails.

Ollie

The doors to Blackburn's office fly open and Rudy's naked and shaved body bursts through and lands on the floor, his corpse birthed through the leather's chrysalis in a clear, sticky gel.

The room flutters with polite applause. The men and women stand up, making delighted exclamations and getting closer to the body.

'Looks like Blackburn's painted himself another portrait,' says one woman who wears a black dress and a white silk shawl. She presses her fingers against Rudy's neck. 'No pulse, everyone!' She pulls a razor out of her purse and tugs on Rudy's ear, cutting the skin beneath it. She holds the ear up in triumph and brings it to her mouth, opening it to accept the blood that drips from the taper of skin she's tugged off with the ear, and she welcomely chews on it.

They crowd the body and bring out their implements to flay and cut and saw their parts off the corpse. There goes Rudy's foot, collected by a waitress on a silver tray to take to the kitchen for cooking. A man obscenely sucks on a blue eye of Rudy's, his mouth forming a new socket for it and it looks

directly at me until he tugs the stringy nerve and vein bundle about with his tongue and the eye looks every which way to the amusement of the other VIPs. He bites down on it and aqueous humor spills down his chin. His partner slips his claws beneath Rudy's scalp, shucking out the skull and slurping the bloody brains through the empty eye socket.

I sit down on one of the leather benches circling a pole. I take my dick out and begin to masturbate and the little gathering of men and women applaud this act of respect for Rudy's corpse. Some approach and ask if they can help me out, and I agree, looking up at the ceiling and crying. Various mouths perform fellatio, bobbing up and down, removing themselves and making space for the next.

I clutch my face in my hands and wail: 'I was gonna get him back! I brought him here to win him back! I was going to make him understand. Kill me, kill me you sick fucks!'

The sucking stops and hands caress my chest.

The guy sodomising Rudy ceases thrusting.

'Oh honey,' a woman says to me, wiping her mouth with a satin glove, 'he was important to you? Take your prize kill! There'll be plenty more for us before the evening's out.'

I'm catatonic as more hands rub all over my surface, trying to bring me back to life.

'I know what he needs,' says an older man with a ring of grey hair. 'He needs to head on upstairs, now!'

'Oh yes!' says a woman at the rear of the circle of people worshiping me. 'If they can't cure an earthly woe, we wouldn't bother.'

I lie back and flop against the bench. The crowd, already having serviced me, remove my boots and socks and jeans and pants and cart me up, and I feel myself rising up along a chain of their bodies in a peristaltic motion of muscles that carts me upwards, out the red room and up above the maze in the main hall, and as the hands spin me, I can see the trapped spaces beyond the maze's path, the bodies pleasuring themselves, the cold corpses erected and trapped in place for easy fucking.

Along the chain I lose the rest of my clothes until I'm upstairs and received by a bouncer who wraps one arm around my waist and carries me around like a simple stack of kindling, and soon I'm on one of the upper floor's many dungeons, many more hands having their way with my body on the journey.

They chain me up against the brick walls and the smell is so familiar: the wet brick, the sweaty bodies. Flashes of memories from my initiation flood my head, but I see them as if floating above my body, looking down upon myself as I commit the most sordid carnal acts with a willingness I'd never shown before.

'I tell you what this lad's problem is,' says a male voice in the darkness in front of me, 'he still has nipples.'

'Yes,' says the voice of an elderly woman, 'what is he thinking, sequestering a delicacy just for himself?'

An index and middle finger pinch behind the steel bar in my left nipple, pulling it forwards, and with the gentleness of a paintbrush stroke, the tugging leaves me and warm blood spills from the hole where the nipple had been, pulsing with the raw strength of my heartbeat.

Pinch, sweep, tug: the right nipple leaves me as well.

Manorites are experts with sharp blades and they leave the gaping holes of my nipples' absences to weep like two bloody eyes while I hear them suck on my severed flesh.

Two thumbs, possibly from the same person, jab themselves into the newly cut holes and I moan in a confused kind of pleasure.

'How does it feel to be free of those?'

The hands smell of heavy cigars.

'Better,' I say.

'We'd love to free you of so much more.'

I have an erection and someone plays with it. Dicks and tits brushed against my skin in the darkness. Use me, use me like

46

Blackburn used Rudy, bring us closer.

I feel my feet bound with metal handcuffs to hoops in the wall.

'Let's get you away from this place that causes you so much pain,' says a gruff male voice, and the tongue of its owner rims my nipple holes.

'Please,' I say. 'I need to start again.'

A thick hand and arm wrap around the small of my back and bring it forwards so my hands and feet are tugged backwards, my body a bridge arching in my spine.

'Mmmmm…'

My back cracks as it's pulled forwards, all the nerves shooting out to the rest of my body, alighting in pain, and the arms tug and jerk at my spine more and more until I'm sure I've been ripped in half and I scream an inhuman scream of some ethereal level of pain, my eyes shutting tightly in the darkness… but soon I feel light, warm orange light that clears the pain and my body drops onto a dusty, warm floor, and it's day again, and I'm free.

Blackburn

I'm nineteen and I've just got out Pete's VW at the Electric Brae. He's taken us both here to look out at the burning dusk.

He puts his hand on my shoulder. 'You've been funny all evening. You've got something to tell me.'

The horrors of my sleep paralysis every night, for one. How they damn me from solitude and company alike. An apparition of you arrives, Pete: he's drenched in blood. He sits on my chest and my mind asks a question that nerves forbid from leaving the mouth: 'Who are you?'

'I love you,' I say.

Glancing my eyes off his soft brow's shadow, I can see he's bemused. 'That's why you can't look at me?' he says.

I'm sweating, cold. I push thumb and finger against the duct tape on the inside of my denim jacket, pressing against the safety razor I taped there before coming out.

'Hey hey hey,' he says. 'I love you too.'

'I don't want you to understand this.'

'There's someone else, right?'

'There's never been anyone else.'

'You're scared, Kingsley. It's not easy to make yourself vulnerable to someone new. I get that. But you have to trust me.'

49

'Do you trust me?'

'Of course.'

My blood-drained fists beat at my temples. I crouch and crunch my knees into my chest with a rapidity that winds me. I'm crying now.

He goes to his trunk to collect a fleecy blanket: it's flaked with festival grass. He wraps me in it with a hug.

'I love that you let me see you like this,' he says. 'I've had suspicions. But this is good.' He finishes with an expression I've tormented myself with for years since: 'Today I begin to understand.'

'We made it this far, Pete. This is where it has to end. I loved you. I loved myself. You loved me, and now you leave me here. Right now.'

'Are you sick?' he says. 'You're drenched. Let me look after you.'

Ball of frozen flesh, dying star: duelling forces keep you stable only for so long.

Pete tries to break my curled, spasming structure. Tries to drag me back to the car. Eyes fixed only on the dead roadside grass, my expression tips him off.

I exude disorder.

My arm stretches out towards Pete, but he's closed the driver door now, rolled up the window almost to the top. I feel it coming.

'Do me one favour, Pete. Please: just one.'

'I would have done anything for you,' he says. 'I can't believe it. How close I was.'

'Remember us as happy.'

I thought I was sick, then. Youth's never been anything worth boasting about.

Slipspace

The day's world was made yellow by the hot sun, filthing up the dirty city air with that summer stench of hot garbage.

Tammy clutched to the merry-go-round pole. Stripped of paint, it was an unromantic metal cast. She felt warmth on her legs, the tailless iron horse heated by the sun already. Her legs were stiff, but she clambered off and tripped down the steps, landing on her hands and knees in hot, dry dirt and dead grass. The fairground had gone. She was in a park now, a park with a broken wooden swing tied with burnt string to corroded poles, a see-saw with bolts eaten by years of wind and rain, a sandpit bordered by splintered wood, a climbing frame with bars that ended mid-rung, broken like old bark.

Above her was a street that undulated San Francisco-style, and on either side of it were burnt houses like she saw last night, bleaching in the sun. Walls were lost, windows smashed, the houses' internals scorched. She'd joined the post-nuclear-holocaust world long ago.

Tammy walked up the street, the wounds of her feet plugging with dust. In cars, in front yards, hanging off the exposed floors of houses, were charred bodies. It frightened her to see how much the skin shrunk when it lost its water, when its components were carbonised by violent levels of radiation. She cried silently.

She heard a shout. At the top of the street was a dark figure waving, a little black ant atop the street's hill. She ducked behind a car, suspecting more trickery. The voice, sharp and dry, called a staccato little 'hey' over and over, like a crow. She leaned her head beyond the car to look up at the figure.

It waved to her.

'I just want to go home!' she cried.

'Tammy?'

'Ollie!'

She emerged from behind the car and staggered up the streets, the bend of her foot as she bore weight on her heel opening up the gashes in her soles, but still she gained speed and ran three, four streets up, and there was Ollie, wearing torn jeans and an open, bloody shirt, revealing two orifices caked with blood where his nipples used to be.

She hugged him gently. He flinched.

'How did you get here?' he said.

'I don't know. You?'

'The Manorites. It was some ritual I wasn't familiar with.'

'Where are we?'

'I don't know. Look.'

He turned Tammy around. Beyond the streets, beyond the play park where Tammy arrived, off in the distance, beneath the yellow sky of beige clouds blending together like an oil painting, close to the shining horizon so close it looked like the sea spilled off into infinity, sparkled a dense and broken concrete city, the windows of its skyscrapers glistening in the yellow of the hot sun. The city was soundless except for the echoing clatter of falling bricks hitting off the sides of mile-high walls, the tap of a crane's winch as it swung in the mild breeze. It was dead, a hollow concrete stack of towering, dusty buildings, and streams of light shot through holes in the buildings and landed on the street. From their distance, it was a model city, with little straw-sized streetlights and bus stops like empty juice cartons.

Just like my nightmares: nothing, no one around. Imagine how many branching basements I can't see, inescapable dungeon-like labyrinths that change configuration with no order at all.

'And look there,' Ollie said.

The city was a circular peninsula in a pink sea, and in the sea were whales the height of the skyscrapers, one to the right and two to the left, almost frozen mid leap, but the way the splashes of water surrounding them sparkled in the sunlight while Tammy and Ollie were still, clearly the whales were crashing in slow motion like a slowly-tilted hologram.

'Is there anyone else?' Tammy said.

'I don't think so. I only got here maybe fifteen minutes before I saw you. Not that I'd know. I was naked. I stripped these clothes from some of the bodies in the houses.'

'Is there more clothing?' She looked at her slashed feet.

'Sure. Let's go find some.'

Ollie put his arm around Tammy's shoulder, and she held his hand around her, and they walked along the dry streets, searching for bodies with clothes to scavenge.

They paced themselves and tried to let the wind's susurration calm them, but instead it fed their shared anxiety.

'H-how long will we be here for?' Tammy said.

'I don't know,' Ollie said.

The body of a woman in a flowery dress was slumped across one of the broken fences. So strange that she had burned and her clothes hadn't.

Ollie helped Tammy lower the body to the floor. He tore the body's dress with his teeth, making strips of fabric that he wound into makeshift shoes for her.

'Thank you.'

'I don't know if we need to walk away from this place or if we're on Earth—'

53

'I don't think so.'

'Or if we can transport ourselves back.'

They walked through the streets until the bodies no longer fazed them: bodies slumped on rooftops, sitting in cars with their hands on the wheel— even though most tires were replaced with bricks— bodies lying on the blackened frames of beds. They gathered clothes, bits of tires and scraps of metal that looked like they could be used for weapons, pieces of wood that could barricade a door. Ollie carried a bike frame on one arm for twenty blocks.

The night came gradually. It was to be a long one—they all were. Long and cold and never quite completely dark, like the blue of my eyes. And sometimes, but not always, they could hear a mechanical and rhythmic grunting sound that echoed from round one of the world's corners.

That first night, Tammy and Ollie dumped their gatherings in the nearest and least ruined house, pushing the bike frame up against the door, testing the stairs to see if they would collapse, and heading into the bedroom. They covered the bare springs of a burnt mattress with the clothes they found and huddled together for warmth.

After three days, their tiredness overcame their fear and they slept.

After two weeks of eating squares of leather, clumps of grass and sipping only from contaminated pools or drinking from the salty sea of the whales, they became hungry enough to try human flesh. They spoke of it with logical language but couldn't look at each other when harvesting thick black jerky from the corpses, gnawing on it. Their stomachs recognised something flavoursome and nutritive enough to ensure their survival, a burnt bacon of sorts, in plentiful supply, for now.

They cried and hugged each other.

'I can't believe we did this! I can't believe we did this!'

'It's okay, Tammy. We had no choice.'

Their bellies ached until they adapted, or sometimes they'd spend whole weeks shitting and vomiting when their bodies became host to worms, bacteria or other parasites, but like dogs their noses soon attuned to the smell of unsafe meat.

They collected meat in the broken fridge of their chosen house. As they stockpiled, they slowly lost their incentive to explore further. But explore further where? Roads led to dust-bowls, toxic deserts, endless seas. Beyond the least scummy pond they drank from, would they chance walking past the eternally burning corpses that stood upright in dry brown fields of grass? Those corpses' eyes never burned: they turned to look at them always. Sometimes, in a flash, all the bodies would be mine, my pale skin untouched by the flames that licked it. I'd look through my brow at them for as long as they could bear it.

They told each other all the stories of their life before. They reminisced about their art school antics. They played hop-scotch in the dirt of their yard, made a backgammon board from their tires, nuts, springs and other parts: neither of them had learned to play in their previous life, and they frequently forgot their own made-up rules.

Their sole form of sexual release for the first two years was masturbation. They did it in front of each other for fear of losing the other, and why not? They pissed and shat and vomited into contaminated waters in front of each other after all.

Even though they huddled together at night, the loneliness was too much. They decided to have sex, comforting one another by saying that they were really thinking of me, as if that was really a comfort: I wasn't coming back.

She got pregnant sometimes but miscarried always throughout her child-bearing years.

Now they were in their eighties, skin slack, cracked and dry, mouths mealy, hair falling out, handfuls of teeth lost to decay and vitamin deficiency, vitality gone. The whales had long since crashed in the water and faded from memory: those corpses that seemed to burn eternally had snuffed out and fallen in the

fields.

The Antlered Saviour

They found me one morning, asleep in the middle of the road outside their house. They were much older, but I was twenty-two, curled up in a pure white onesie with buttons down the front, the big branches of male antlers grown from my forehead.

I woke up in Tammy's arms as she shook me wildly back and forth, licking at my neck, howling.

Ollie came running out after her with a knife whittled from a rib, which he dropped to the floor as he joined our embrace.

'Ohhh!' Tammy said, 'his clothes are so clean!'

'And his skin is so fresh and pure,' Ollie said, stroking my face with wonder. 'The colour of a cool, delicious glass of milk. I want to bite him.'

I could recognise them by their eyes, faded as they were. But Tammy's hair was long and grey, dry grass tangled in its ends. Her face lacked the sauciness it once had. Ollie was slim and gaunt, skin ashy with dust and dead flakes, hairline receded and what remained of his hair grew out in clumps like a big eyelash at the back of his head. He slouched, his belly pouting forwards, his nipples replaced by keloid scars like dead cherry tomatoes.

'Listen carefully,' Tammy said, 'you need to tell us exactly how you got here. Maybe there's some clue to getting us out?'

'No,' I said.

She wailed desperately as if that was the end of my answer.

'I've been trying for a very very long time to come here: don't you understand?'

'Are you saying that you know where we are?' Ollie said.

I nodded. 'This,' I said, gesturing around, 'is the landscape of Blackburn's mind.'

'His mind?'

'Look.' I pointed up to where I had smashed through its ceiling, nothing but a scratch in the clouds where we were. I stroked the hair of both of them when I saw how much it strained them to see where I was looking, their eyesight not as good as it was. 'That night, the night of the Bonespin, I had an out-of-body experience. At first I was in ecstasy: my infinite mind freed from my body. But as I floated above myself, I saw I'd been tricked. Blackburn wanted my body. And he'd locked me out of it. I had to hover above and watch how he mutilated it, choked it, beat, brutalised and fucked it.'

Tammy wailed, placing a hand over her mouth.

'You didn't know?' I said. 'Neither of you? That my physical self died?'

'No,' Ollie said. 'We didn't know.'

'Once it was done with, the reality of Blackburn's office extinguished, and I was alone and trapped in a slim, dark, infinite corridor. Like,' I pointed to Ollie, 'like the walls behind that maze!' I bit the skin of my thumb in thought. 'I walked for days in one direction, days in the other. I couldn't bend my knees, couldn't lie down. I spent almost as long as you've been here in that corridor, in agonising pain.'

'How did you get free?' Tammy asked.

'Today, I could sense your weakness, for the first time ever. I closed my eyes and envisioned myself kneeling down and pulling up a sack of sparkling light over my body. Once the light enveloped me, I could walk free. Just like that I was apart from the world in which I had existed, and I rose up, closing my eyes and thinking of your both, and so I saw Blackburn beneath me, the top of his skull removed and replaced with a translucent dome, and as I fell and he got bigger, in that dome was a world, and that world was here, so I fell and with all my force I smashed through the dome and landed where you were, in this street here, in my ball of yellow light.'

'Oh, Rudy…' Tammy said. They hugged me again.

'I just wish you could have come sooner,' Ollie said. 'And I'm so sorry for what you went through.'

'Well, Blackburn drew strength from you during this time,' I said. 'You had to weaken before I could come here. Where I was didn't have the same rules. It wasn't a man's mind. It wasn't anywhere. It was a limbo, a waiting line. Nothing could have happened any sooner. So let's not dwell on it more.'

'Tell us what you know about this place,' Ollie said. 'Is there anyone else here?'

'There certainly is,' I said. 'But no one you'd want to meet.'

'Is there a way out?' Tammy said.

'Of course. I'll take us there now.'

As if they'd been tazed, they fell to their knees and cried out with the relief of a life, lived in anguish, ended.

'Why did we never find it?' Tammy said. 'The days we spent in the empty city, climbing up the skyscrapers on makeshift ladders and finding nothing but a floor of living mannequins at the top or lynched alligators hanging from bent beams. The distances we swam through the seas! The depths we dug into the dead soil!'

'The one place you didn't try,' I said.

'The toxic desert,' Ollie said.

I nodded again. 'Please don't worry: there's no way you would have made it. Your spirits would have died in its poisonous sands, and that wouldn't have done any of us any good at all. In your toil, you allowed yourselves to be reborn. We have a place back on Earth, a purpose there. Now let's return.'

He knew we were here. The earth rumbled, the ground beneath us split and muddy water bubbled out in streams. Tammy screamed and curled into a ball on the floor. Ollie hugged onto me and held me to the ground. The houses shook so hard some fell on their sides. Cars careened towards us. The city down below filled with clouds of dust as spires collapsed and floors fell down on floors below, and its island tilted and inverted, the city drowned in the deep, replaced by a tall brown mountain.

Ollie and Tammy lowered their heads. I stood up and pinched the backs of their necks like a mother cat, accepting them into my pellucid sphere of yellow light, and I flew up and carted them across the toxic desert.

Journey to the Spire

We hurtled across the sands, Tammy and Ollie sliding together in the base of my light's sphere. We sped low over the desert so they could feel the winds plinking grains against my ball of light, a sandstorm blowing across a window. The sands vibrated like they'd been poured onto a loudspeaker. Yellow silica blended into the deep purple of permanganate, miles into our journey, and the purple begat a field of oiled caesium that popped and exploded in violent fireworks when the particles were touched with condensation. I was fairly sure my shield could protect my friends from the irradiated wastelands, but their spirits were too old for them to live long enough and feel the side effects of any moderate dosage anyway.

I took our path on a gentle incline so they slipped into the base of the ball, and high above we could see the full circular rim of Blackburn's head, how the light caught and revealed the shape of the artificial sky's dome.

'Do you see it?' I said.

A spire grew out of the distance, steely grey against the purple sky as a long night came upon us.

'It's a tower.' Tammy said.

'A tower in the centre of his mind,' I said.

'I guess we need to get to the top?' Ollie said.

'I'd guess the same,' I said.

'Wait, then why are you taking us back down?'

'It's not me!'

'It's okay, Rudy,' Tammy said. 'I felt something like this before I came here. I think once you get close to some building or room Blackburn wants to draw you towards, invisible walls narrow your path.'

That was probably it. I was losing lift, and I tried to guide us free of the wall that was forcing us down, but I encountered an invisible cone of it, centring on some building at the spire's base down below.

As we descended, our view now was all dark desert, all around. The horizon was a glowing yellow corona, spikes of the crown's light shooting up in curves through the clear and purple sky. We were close to the spire now. It was as thick as a city. Tubes jutting out its walls belched flames into the night. Slim windows revealed big factory floors in white light with red and white warning tape on the sharp edges of boxes, plinths and staircases. Black rubber boots paced themselves along the floors with zombie-like gaits. Levels below exuded a lusty red: vintage Turkish rugs were spread across black-painted floors, layered on top of each other in large heaps; red leather chaises and burgundy velvet recamiers with solid gold claw feet clustered in the room and stacked on top of one another: there was no way of having gotten them all into the room and definitely no way of getting any of them back out. Other rooms were barren, concrete, unlit. Some windows had a level of dirty pond water bobbing against them. Some levels were as high as skyscrapers, as we could see through several thick bands of windows, and inside were what I might describe as attempts by some randomising computer to build a city: several identical and empty Greek temples pressed against each other in one corner behind a floor-to-ceiling hospital; a beach lined with

Mercedes cars in a showroom display; an endless shrine, grow-
ing like a fungus from one corner of the room and across the
windows and up the walls, with candles running all across its
surface, and on the ceiling the candles had flames that pointed
downwards. Further down: an empty, mouldy hotel floor; rows
of naked people standing like soldiers, all facing a blank wall;
an enormous shower head taking over the ceiling of a flood-
ed room; a spotlight-flooded cube of spotty skin, sporadically
haired, that seemed to breathe.

What all these rooms and levels, these visions, had in com-
mon, was that they all contained recognisable objects, spaces,
structures, concepts, ideas taken from life, but always used in a
misunderstood pattern. It was the home of evil.

The invisible cone of wall brought us down to a metal slope
that led to a bunker's entrance. I released my sphere of light
and we hugged our shoulders as the cold desert wind blew
against us.

We walked towards the door. I pressed my hand against it and
it slid open to reveal a tunnel in pure darkness, which we three
soundlessly entered.

Large white strip-lights of all sizes hovered in the air at a
strange angle, or were impaled through the floor, ceiling or
wall and buzzed loudly. Some were so small that they brushed
past our cheek or hands as they dangled from near-invisible
steel cords. Others were so large that they nearly occluded the
hallway, and we had to duck to enter the triangle of space it left
beside one wall. The light was so strong, we could feel the heat
coming off it, so we tried desperately not to touch the glass,
which would surely burn us. With care, we made it to the end
of the hallway and the slope brought us back up and into a
factory at the spire's base.

Ollie slipped a rib-knife out of a tube he'd sewn into the
inside of his sleeve. He pulled up his shirt at the back and removed two large rusty shards of metal and handed one to me
and one to Tammy. The shards had sliced long, oozing streaks

of red out of his back.

The factory floor was filled with large storage containers, all painted white, with the red and white tape spread across them randomly. Some were completely covered, some were only taped around their borders, and some had no tape at all. Their configuration was again a roll-of-the-dice-style pattern, as was the walking pattern of the guards and workers whose boots could be heard echoing off the walls. Tap, tap, tap. They wore white radiation suits and black boots, but their heads—if they had them—were those of pigs, and they bled continuously, streaming down the suits and smattering the floors.

'I believe there is a safe path for us,' I whispered.

'To where?' Ollie asked.

'A lift can take us to the top.'

'Where is it? This floor looks endless!' Tammy said.

'A maze,' I said. 'Right? An invisible maze will guide us through. Just as it guided you here, Tammy.'

'If it brought Tammy here, we can't trust its guidance!' Ollie said.

'I think we can. You saw all the stuff he's gathered in this spire, right? Blackburn directs just as much towards a worse place as he does to a better place. He seems entirely indifferent to either. But if he offers any guidance through this place, I believe it will take us to the lift.'

We walked, hand-in-hand, in the shadows of the containers, and sure enough, as we timed our running between shadows, we were guided in directions we didn't know we needed, to further away shadows. At one point, all directions seemed blocked off until Ollie tried to climb and found invisible steps that took us to a height several containers up, and from there, in the very centre of the room, we saw a black cylinder with a split from which light poured. Guards with rifles circled it like it was their Mecca, forming dense loops that walked in opposite directions from one another. Or, they walked into walls, their boots sliding on the floor as if they expected to carry on

in their path where they'd hit the wall. Some guards had no arms; some had no legs. Some had assault rifles and even more just had randomly configured assault rifle parts and some even mimed as if they held an assault rifle while a magazine of bullets floated beneath their arms.

'But I'm sure that...' I said.

Ollie and Tammy held onto one of my hands and I leaned out over the container's lip, feeling around. A sensation like the static fuzz on a plastic slide brought my hand to an invisible tube with a gentle slope in the cylinder's direction. I stepped a foot out onto it and lowered myself, still while Tammy and Ollie held me, so that I was lying on an invisible plane beyond the container. We formed a chain and slid further into the tube, with Ollie clutching Tammy's hand and lying on his belly, his feet the last thing to leave the container as we slid in our invisible path above the guards. Those with the faculties to notice us did, and they stood in their spots and shot their rifles at us, but only few rifles fired: most just clicked. Blind guards with working rifles turned to the source of the noise and gunned down the shooting guards where they stood. They resumed their path around the cylinder.

We landed at the cylinder and its surface spread backwards in a wave, like a millipede bending its legs back, and on the inner silvery surface were more lights, and at the bottom of the cylinder was a circular piece of metal. We stood on the circle and it whirred us upwards.

Through the lift, each floor we saw, even with every indication that we'd just seen it from the outside, was now barren concrete, sometimes with a string of wire or two, sometimes with a bulb, sometimes just a sparking tip lying in a puddle.

We held each other tightly on the off chance that there was no barrier beyond the circle of metal we stood upon, and we shifted about to try and stop our legs from aching as the lift took us up, up, up until there wasn't much night left, and the sky was turning orange, edging out the purple.

Each floor narrowed to the needle tip that was the top of the spire. As the lift stopped at the top floor, we fell out onto black velvet.

It was a control room no bigger than the size of an office, with a few metal stools like those in Blackburn's office and a wide control desk bordering the cone of clear glass that made up the room's walls. Up here we could still hear the wind blowing, oooooOOoOoooo...

Tammy tugged at her hair and clumps of it slid out too easily. 'Fuck! We don't know what the hell these controls are for!'

'We don't need to touch them,' I said.

'No,' Ollie said. 'Now, we need to fuck.'

We pushed the chairs out the way to give ourselves enough space on the floor, and we stripped off our clothes. I got hard instantly. Ollie was hard sooner after me than I expected, his dick bending out of a grey moss. We helped him lay down on the floor and there he stayed for the act, while Tammy and I changed positions on top of him, pleasuring him, each other, fucking on top of him, fucking him, going through every permutation of the performance we could think of, and slowly the bag of light that arrived so brightly in my corridor before I came here bordered us in the cone-like shape of a tipi, and we smiled until the light was so bright that we could no longer see each other at all, and we were bones hanging from the roof of so many tents in the Manor's yard, glowing and protecting the carnal acts that took place within, and soon, from the release of so many other good souls from the barren minds of sadistic debutantes, we claimed all the bones throughout the entire graveyard, and we vibrated with our combined power and glowed white hot, and the demons fucking beneath us screamed in pleasure and pain as shards of searing bone burst across them as we angels escaped our physical forms, our spirits burrowing through the graveyard's grounds and carving out the dirt and stone of the manor's foundation, and we tore the block of it from its moorings and thrust it upwards until at

69

great speed the manor burned through the air, the object's tip spreading out a fierce fire like a rocket coming home, we angels using the ground we'd torn for a shield as bricks and stones and clumps of dirt accelerated past us, and as the manor and the graveyard and the dirt and the stone disintegrated before us, we were free, and we carried on through the skies, up towards Heaven.

Acknowledgements

Leo X. Robertson:

Thanks to Marc Molino and Thuy Vi Pham for their awesome artistic contributions and for putting up with my chat in general: if there were such a thing as "too kind", they'd be it.

Thanks also to Tracy Reilly for allowing herself to be haunted by this piece and, assuming it was out of compassion rather than inconvenience, for not causing me any harm afterwards.

Thanks to author Rebecca Gransden for being the first official reader of this piece, for reassuring me that I didn't need to justify having written it and for so many other things I can't even express in words.

Thanks to my family for agreeing not to read this and to my husband, Mr Juan Rojas, for not judging me.

Biggest thanks of all to Psychedelic Horror Press for taking a chance on me!

Psychedelic Horror Press:

Thanks to Marc Molino for the devastating cover, Thuy Vi Pham for the stark and eerie images, and to Leo X. Robertson for his endless patience, commitment, diligence, and fearlessness!

About the Author

Leo X. Robertson is a Scottish process engineer and writer, currently living in Oslo, Norway. In addition to this novella, he has work published by *Unnerving, Twisted50, Schlock!* and *The Stockholm Review of Literature*, amongst others. Follow him on Twitter @Leoxwrite or find out news of his latest publications at leoxrobertson.wordpress.com

The Golden Psycho Psychedelic Horror Press Library

PHP 001 *Governor of the Homeless* by G. Arthur Brown
PHP 002 *Bonespin Slipspace* by Leo X. Robertson